Poodle
and the Pea

written by Charlotte Guillain ☆ illustrated by Dawn Beacon

Raintree

Raintree is an imprint of Capstone Global Library Limited, a company incorporated in England and Wales having its registered office at 7 Pilgrim Street, London, EC4V 6LB – Registered company number: 6695582

To contact Raintree please phone 0845 6044371, fax + 44 (0) 1865 312263, or email myorders@raintreepublishers.co.uk. Customers from outside the UK please telephone +44 1865 312262.

Edited by Daniel Nunn, Rebecca Rissman, and Sian Smith
Designed by Joanna Hinton-Malivoire
Original illustrations © Capstone Global Library Ltd 2013
Illustrated by Dawn Beacon
Production by Victoria Fitzgerald
Originated by Capstone Global Library Ltd
Printed in China

ISBN 978 1 406 25117 3
16 15 14 13 12
10 9 8 7 6 5 4 3 2 1

This book is also available as a big book with the ISBN: 978 1 406 25123 4

British Library Cataloguing in Publication Data
Guillain, Charlotte.
   The poodle and the pea. -- (Animal fairy tales)
   1. Children's stories.
   I. Title II. Series
   823.9'2-dc23

Characters

Princess Poodle

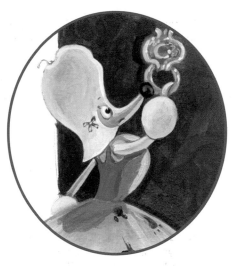

Prince Barking

king and queen

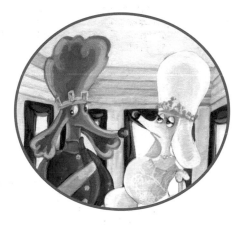

princesses

servant

Once upon a time, a king and queen lived in a fine palace. They had one son, Prince Barking.

One day, the king and queen told Prince Barking it was time for him to get married.

Many princesses came to the palace to
meet the prince.

But the prince didn't want to marry
any of them.

That night, a young princess was lost
in the forest near the palace.

She was cold, tired, and scared.

At last, she stumbled out of the forest and saw the palace. She knocked on the door.

A servant let her in and took her to the
king and queen. She thanked them and
told them she was a lost princess.

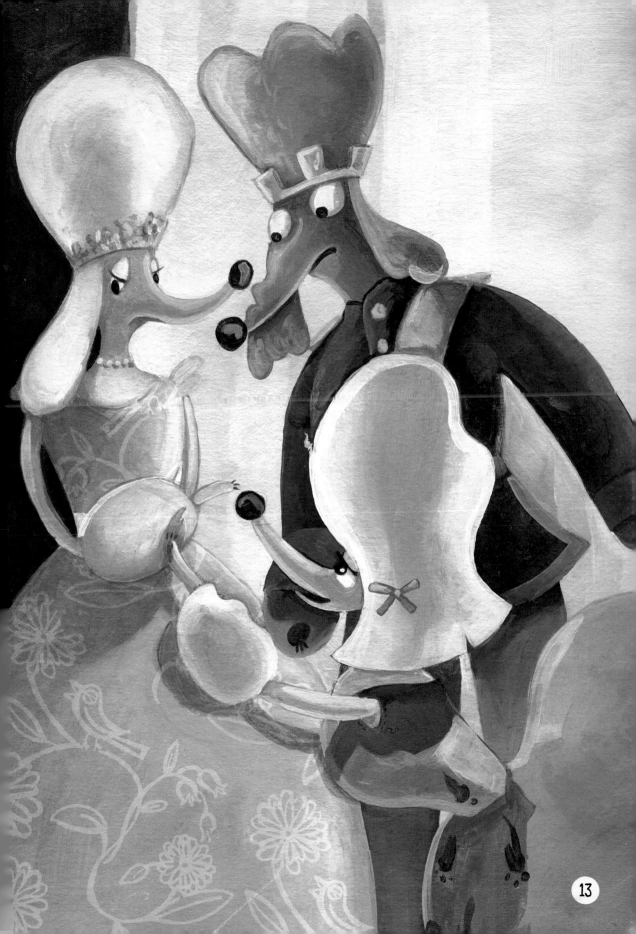

The king and queen didn't believe anyone so dirty and bedraggled could be a princess. But the prince liked her.

Then the servant had an idea.

The servant put a pea in a bed and piled blankets on top of it.

"Let her sleep in this basket tonight," he said. "In the morning, we will know if she is truly a princess."

The princess wearily climbed to the top
of the blankets. Then she curled up and
tried to sleep.

When morning came, the princess
hadn't slept at all. She complained that
her bed had been lumpy.

"Aha!" said the king. "Only a real
princess could feel a pea under all
those blankets!"

Prince Barking was delighted! He asked the princess to marry him and at their wedding feast there were piles of peas for everyone!

The end

Where does this story come from?

You've probably already heard the story that *The Poodle and the Pea* is based on — *The Princess and the Pea*. There are many different versions of this story. When people tell a story, they often make little changes to make it their own. How would you change this story?

The history of the story

The Princess and the Pea story was written by Hans Christian Andersen. Andersen was born in 1805 and lived in Denmark. He wrote many poems and stories, including many fairy tales. Andersen's fairy stories became famous around the world.

The original story is called *The Princess and the Pea*. A prince is looking for a princess to marry but he can't find the right girl. He's also not sure if everyone he meets really is a princess. On a stormy night, a bedraggled girl arrives at the palace. When she says she's a princess, the prince's mother puts a pea in the girl's bed and covers it with 20 mattresses and 20 featherbeds. This is a test to see if she really is a princess.

In the morning, the princess complains that something hard in the bed stopped her from sleeping. She has passed the test — only a real princess could be so sensitive! The prince marries her and they put the pea in a museum.